NIKO Draws a Feeling

Bob Raczka

illustrations by
Simone Shin

CAROLRHODA BOOKS • MINNEAPOLIS

To those who color outside the lines
—B.R.

To Laura, a wonderful artist, teacher, and friend
—S.S.

Carolrhoda Books
A division of Lerner Publishing Group, Inc.
241 First Avenue North
Minneapolis, MN 55401 USA

For reading levels and more information, look up this title at www.lernerbooks.com.

Designed by Danielle Carnito.
Main body text set in Sunshine Regular 21/26. Typeface provided by Chank.
The illustrations in this book were created using mixed media, digital, and acrylic paint.

Library of Congress Cataloging-in-Publication Data

Names: Raczka, Bob, author. | Shin, Simone, illustrator.
Title: Niko draws a feeling / by Bob Raczka ; illustrated by Simone Shin.
Description: Minneapolis : Carolrhoda Books, [2017] | Summary: "No one understands the abstract pictures that Niko draws until a new friend sees the thought and feeling within his shapes and forms" —Provided by publisher.
Identifiers: LCCN 2015044789| ISBN 9781467798433 (lb : alk. paper) | ISBN 9781512426885 (eb pdf)
Subjects: | CYAC: Drawing—Fiction.
Classification: LCC PZ7.1.R33 Ni 2017 | DDC [E]—dc23

LC record available at https://lccn.loc.gov/2015044789

Manufactured in the United States of America
2-44110-20692-4/19/2017

Niko loved to make pictures.
Everywhere he went, he carried a box
of colored pencils and a pad of paper.

Because everywhere he
looked, he saw something
that inspired him.

It might be a mother bird building her nest.

Or the low autumn sun peeking out from behind a cloud.

Or the ice cream truck ring-a-linging down the street.

When Niko was inspired,
it felt like a window
opening in his brain.

An idea would flit through the
open window like a butterfly,
flutter down to his stomach,

then along his arm and fingers to his pencils,

where it would escape onto his paper in a whirlwind of color.

It was a wonderful feeling,
and Niko tried to capture
it as often as he could.

Sometimes he showed his pictures to his friends.

"What is it?" one of them would ask.

"It's the ring-a-ling of the ice cream truck," Niko would answer.

"It doesn't look like the ice cream truck," someone else would say.

"It's not the ice cream truck," Niko would explain. "It's the ring-a-ling."

"Where's the bell?"

"It's not the bell. It's the ring-a-ling."

"I don't get it."

Sometimes he showed his pictures to his parents.

"What is it?" his mom would ask.

"It's the warm of the sun on my face," Niko would answer.

"I don't see the sun," his dad would say.

"It's not the sun. It's the warm."

"Where's your face?"

"It's not my face. It's the warm."

"Oh."

Once he showed a picture to his teacher, Miss Reed.

"What is it?" Miss Reed asked.

"It's the hard work of a mother robin building her nest," Niko answered.

"Where's the robin?"

"It's not a robin. It's her hard work."

"So this is the nest?"

"It's not the nest. It's her hard work."

"I see."

But Miss Reed didn't see. None of them did.

One night, Niko sat on his bed thinking about all the pictures taped to his walls.

Then he looked at himself in the mirror.

He was inspired to make another picture, only this one he taped to the back of his door, where no one else could see it.

The next day, Niko was heading out with his paper and colored pencils when he noticed a moving truck next door—and a girl about his age.

"Hi," said the girl. "I'm Iris."

"I'm Niko. Hi."

"What are you doing with that stuff?"

"This? Nothing."

"Are you going to draw?"

"Well, yeah. I like to make pictures."

"Can I see them?"

"I don't know," he said. "You might not like them."

"But I might," Iris answered.

Niko decided it would
be rude to say no, so
he invited Iris over.

When they got to his
room, Niko waited
for her questions.

But she just looked and looked.

Finally, after looking at every picture in the room, Iris discovered the one behind the door.

"Wow," said Iris.

"What?" said Niko.

"You must have
been sad when you
made this picture."

"How did
you know?"

Iris thought. "It looks
like how I feel. You
know, sad because I
had to move."

Suddenly, Niko felt
a window opening in
his brain.

"Can I make a picture for you?" asked Niko.

"For me?
Sure!"
said Iris.

Like a butterfly, an idea flitted through the open window,

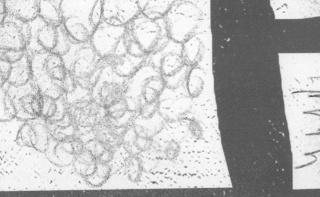

fluttered down to his stomach,
then along his arm and fingers to his colored pencils,
where it escaped onto his
paper in a whirlwind of color.

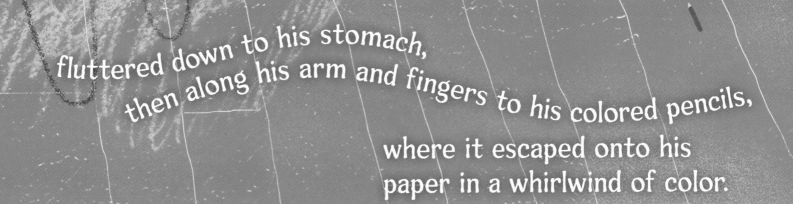

When he was finished, he
handed the picture to Iris.

This time, Niko asked the question.

"What is it?"

Iris looked at the picture for a long time without saying a word. At last, she looked up at Niko.

"I'm not sure exactly,
but it makes me feel like
I made a new friend."

Niko stared at Iris.

"You can see that?"

"I can feel it," Iris replied, "like a butterfly landing on my finger."

"A butterfly?" asked Niko.

"I know, it sounds weird."

Niko smiled.

"Not to me."